Escape the
TWISTER

Stephanie Dagg

MENTOR
BOOKS

This Edition first published 2003 by

MENTOR BOOKS
43 Furze Road,
Sandyford Industrial Estate,
Dublin 18.

Tel. (01) 295 2112/3   Fax. (01) 295 2114
email: admin@mentorbooks.ie

ISBN: 1-84210-198-6

Cover Illustration: Nicola Sedgwick
Typesetting, editing, design and layout by Mentor Books

Printed in Ireland by ColourBooks

1 3 5 7 9 10 8 6 4 2

CONTENTS

The Author

Stephanie Dagg

Stephanie Dagg lives near Bandon in County Cork.

She is married to Chris and is the mother of three children, Benjamin, Caitlín and Ruadhrí and has been writing stories ever since she was a child. Originally from Suffolk in England, she moved to Cork in 1992.

Dedicated to
the memory of Christine Gallagher
16.12.1956 – 18.10.2001

We are so lucky
to have known you, Christine

1. News

'What did you just say?' Kevin Murphy's voice over the phone was shrill with excitement.

Tom Donoghue grinned in delight. He'd just surprised the socks off his best friend.

'You heard. But I'll tell you again anyway. Mum says do you want to come to America with us next month when we go and see Alan?'

There was an almighty crash as the receiver at Kevin's end thudded to the floor. Kevin had let it drop as he ran off to find his mother to ask her permission. Tom fidgeted impatiently for a few minutes until he heard a pounding of feet, deep breathing and an assortment of crunchy crackly noises as Kevin arrived back at the phone and picked it up.

'Mum says you must be mad to want to take me,' he panted happily. 'She'll talk to your mum tomorrow to sort out money and stuff. She said it's probably OK so long as it's not too dear. Is it? Dear, I mean.'

'Don't panic,' Tom told him. 'Mum's got loads of air miles to use up. She's been saving them up for ages. She reckons the travel will hardly cost anything. And we'll be staying with Alan in the apartment he's renting. So Mum says there will only be food to pay for. Mind you, in your case, that could be expensive.'

Kevin was famous for his huge appetite for chips and burgers.

'True!' replied Kevin good naturedly. He hardly ever got narky. 'But wow, this is so cool! I've always wanted to go to America!'

'Yeah, me too!' agreed Tom.

'Do you think we'll see some car chases like on telly?' said Kevin. 'There must be loads every day in America.'

'Bound to,' gushed Tom. 'And police shoot-outs, I bet.'

'Wicked.' Both boys sighed happily at the prospect.

'Tom, tea's ready,' Mum called from the kitchen.

'Oh, got to go,' groaned Tom. 'See you tomorrow.'

'OK, bye then. And thanks again for the

invite!' Kevin hung up.

Tom galloped down the hall to the kitchen, grinning like a moron.

'I don't need to ask what Kevin said,' smiled Mum, setting out bowls of soup.

'His mum said "Yes" so long as it's not too dear,' Tom reported, slipping into his place.

'Did you—?' began Mum.

'Yup, I told him about the air miles and everything,' Tom nodded. 'Mrs Murphy said she will give you a ring tomorrow.'

'That's great,' said Mum.

'It will be fun with Kevin,' agreed Anna, Tom's little sister.

'I don't think school will mind you guys missing two weeks,' observed Mum. 'It'll be educational, after all. Alan's going to show you the caves where he's doing all his research, and we'll take in some museums and exhibitions.'

'We will?' Tom stopped slurping soup for a moment. He wasn't sure he liked the sound of that. Weren't museums just full of dead stuffed animals and bits of broken pottery?

'Don't worry,' Mum reassured him, seeing the look on his face. 'Alan has told me all about this

9

amazing science museum with loads of hands-on things for kids. And there's some robot exhibition as well, he says. Oh, and there's a dog museum!'

Tom relaxed. Anna smiled happily at the mention of dogs.

'And there are some wonderful shopping malls, too, apparently' added Mum. 'We can shop till we drop!'

'Like we do when we go to those huge supermarkets in France?' asked Tom.

Mum nodded. 'I've always wanted to go to a shopping mall.'

'Me too,' agreed Anna. She wasn't actually sure what a shopping mall was, but if Mum wanted to go, then so did she.

'A trip like this is just what we need after our last few crazy holidays.' Mum shuddered as she thought back to their previous experiences of a volcanic eruption, an avalanche and a flood. 'I'm looking forward to a nice, relaxing break in a quiet, civilised town.'

'Yes, we only ever seem to have adventures in France so it's bound to be dead quiet in America,' agreed Tom.

'Perfect,' smiled Mum. 'Just perfect.'

2. Flying High

'Just how cool is this plane!' said Kevin, for about the hundredth time, and they hadn't even taken off yet.

He and Tom looked around and sighed with contentment. They were sitting, with Mum and Anna, in the centre four seats of the Airbus A330. To the right and left of them were aisles, beyond them were two more seats next to the windows. The plane seemed to stretch for miles behind and in front of them. It was huge. But what impressed the boys most was the large video screen on the wall that sectioned off the business class cabin.

'This is ace!' grinned Kevin. 'TV all the way to America! What d'you think, Mrs D?' Kevin always called Tom's mum that.

'Well, it's a very nice plane,' said Mum, rather doubtfully. 'But I'm sure it must be too heavy to take off.'

'It weighs 230 tonnes,' Tom told her.

'Goodness,' said Mum faintly.

'Also, it's 63.6 metres long, 5.28 metres wide,

the fuel tank holds 97,530 litres and the engines give up to 72,000 pounds of thrust.' Tom rattled off a list of figures with a superior smile.

'Hey look, it's Professor Know-All!' teased Kevin, but actually he was very impressed. 'How do you know all that?'

'I looked it up on the Airbus website last night,' Tom told him.

'I looked too,' said Anna.

'This is one of the most advanced civil aeroplanes,' Tom concluded.

'Wow!' said Kevin. 'You know, maybe I'll go for a job as a flight attendant when I leave school.'

'Nah, those green dresses they wear wouldn't suit you,' joked Tom.

'Ha ha,' replied Kevin. 'You do get male flight attendants, you know.'

'I think they like to be called cabin crew members these day,' said Mum. 'Oh look, here are some now. We must be taking off fairly soon.'

Two smartly dressed women were coming down the aisles. One was handing out copies of the in-flight magazine and the other was handing out boiled sweets from a small wicker basket. Anna greedily took a handful. Mum tut-tutted crossly but the cabin crew member smiled.

'Don't eat them yet,' warned Mum. 'Wait till we've started to taxi down the runway. You want to be sucking them for the take-off so your ears don't go pop.'

'Hey, this is a bit different from the last time we went flying, isn't it?' said Kevin suddenly. 'We were in a tiny plane then.'

'Yes, that Cherokee during our avalanche adventure in France, you mean,' nodded Tom. 'There's a bit more leg room in this plane!'

'I think I preferred the Cherokee,' murmured Mum. 'It was nice and light.'

'Oh Mrs D! Don't be silly. You heard Tom, this plane has got mega-enormous engines with zillions of pounds of thrust. We'll probably go into orbit!' Kevin reassured her.

Mum went a bit green.

A cabin crew member came past again, this time checking that the seats were upright and any hand luggage was out of the way.

'Wicked!' said Kevin, and settled back to enjoy the trip.

3. Forty-Eight Flavours

'Is it really only four o'clock, Mum?' Tom had known about the five-hour time difference between Ireland and the east coast of America — he'd spent ages trying to explain about it to Anna before they'd set off. But now it was real, and it was weird. His body told him it was bedtime, but his surroundings clearly spelt out that it was the middle of the afternoon.

'Yes, four o'clock,' Mum assured him wearily.

They were standing by the carousel in the arrivals hall, waiting for their luggage to appear.

'Oh look, there's my bag,' yawned Kevin as he stumbled forwards to grab it.

'You've made me yawn now,' grumbled Tom, yawning and stretching too.

'Goodness, what a bunch of sleepyheads we all are,' said Mum.

'I'm not tired,' Anna told her. She'd slept for most of the journey.

'Bully for you,' snapped Tom.

'Enough!' warned Mum sharply. 'Let's not

start our holiday on a bad note. There's my green case. Mind Anna, please Tom, while I get it.'

Tom reluctantly took his little sister's sticky hand. Her hands were always sticky.

Their other case soon trundled round on the carousel so Mum grabbed that too.

'OK, all set! Let's go and find Alan.' She smiled happily as she began to wheel the trolley along. Anna bounced along beside her. Even Tom and Kevin found a new burst of energy. It would be nice to see Alan again. It was three months since they'd seen him. Alan was Mum's boyfriend and he was going to be Tom and Anna's new dad soon. They were engaged to be married but hadn't set a date yet. Alan, who lived in England, was still trying to find a job in Ireland. He was in America for six months, doing some research for the university he worked for as a cave scientist, a speleologist. They'd first met Alan during their volcano adventure in France.

A sea of faces met them as they came through the arrivals gate.

'What a lot of people!' gasped Mum. 'We'll never find Alan!'

'Yes we will. I can see him!' Anna pointed into

the crowd.

Sure enough, there he was. Or at least, there was the top of his head just showing over a huge bunch of flowers and a bundle of parcels. Mum charged towards him with the trolley. Anna galloped ahead of her and got the first hug, but Mum got the longest!

'Oh, it's so good to see you guys!' cried Alan happily, handing out gifts. Mum got the flowers, Anna got a huge Winnie the Pooh teddy, and Tom and Kevin got baseball hats and sweatshirts.

'Not that you'll need to wear those tops at the moment,' Alan told them. 'The weather's beautiful.' He took the trolley from Mum and pushed it along. 'You're going to love St Denis. It's a swell city.'

'You sound American,' giggled Anna.

'Do I?' said Alan. 'Well, I bet you guys will too after a couple of weeks here. But first things first, and if I know the Donoghues and the Murphys, then what we need now is food.'

'Oh, not for me,' groaned Mum. 'All we seemed to do was eat on the way over. I won't need another meal for weeks!'

'Mrs D, all we got were a few mouthfuls,'

16

Kevin corrected her. 'And it was all weird stuff.'

'He means it wasn't chips,' explained Tom, with a grin.

'Like I said, weird,' nodded Kevin.

'And our blood coca-cola levels are way down too,' added Tom. 'They only give you these tiny little drinks cans on the plane.'

'I'd love an ice cream,' said Anna.

'OK, let's eat then,' smiled Alan. 'Here's ice cream for Anna.' He stopped the trolley outside a large ice cream parlour. Deliciously cold air swirled out to meet them. 'Who's coming in?'

'I'll come,' said Kevin. 'I can force an ice cream down.'

'Jane?' Alan asked Mum.

'No, I'll stay with the trolley,' she answered.

'I'll stay too,' said Tom.

'OK, we shan't be a minute.' Alan, Anna and Kevin headed inside.

About ten minutes later they finally emerged with huge cardboard cartons full of ice cream.

'What took so long?' asked Mum.

'There were forty-eight flavours to choose from,' explained Kevin. 'It was very hard to decide.'

'Forty-eight? How can you get forty-eight flavours of ice cream?' Tom was amazed.

'Easy,' shrugged Kevin. 'There's all the usual boring ones, then mega-tons of these really cool ones, like pecan and maple, cookies and cream, blueberry and meringue, butternut and popcorn – that kind of thing!'

'Wow, what have you got?' demanded Tom.

'Dogfood and doughnut, want to try it?' laughed Kevin, holding out a spoonful.

'What is it really?' asked Mum.

'No idea,' admitted Kevin.

'I got fed up waiting for them to make up their minds, you see,' confessed Alan, 'so in the end I asked the assistant to give them a few different flavours each.'

'Good thinking,' said Mum.

'I've mixed all mine up together,' said Kevin. 'It tastes great!'

'Mmm, it does, doesn't it!' agreed Tom, licking the finger that he'd just dunked into Kevin's carton.

They all stood and shared the ice cream. In the end, Mum ate most of Anna's.

'I thought you weren't hungry,' objected Tom.

'I'm not, I'm just greedy!' smiled Mum. 'This stuff is irresistible.'

'And so are you.' Alan gave Mum a kiss.

'What about me? Am I irresistible too?' grinned Kevin.

'That's not the first word that springs to mind when I think about Kevin Murphy!' teased Alan. 'Come on, let's find something to drink.'

They came across a row of vending machines that seemed to sell just about everything under the sun. Alan had a pocketful of change so they ended up with several icy-cold cans of coke, a St Denis Airport souvenir keyring, some travel tissues (to clean up Anna's ice-creamy chin), some powerful aspirin for Mum (whose head was beginning to throb with all the noise and bustle in the airport), and chewing gum for everyone.

'Let's get you home now,' said Alan, noticing that they were all starting to wilt, even after a refreshing drink. 'We'll start the sightseeing tomorrow.'

4. Sightseeing

They all surfaced very late the next day. Mum needed several strong cups of coffee to get her eyes to open properly. The children were snappy and grumpy to start with, but after a couple of bowls each of a very chocolaty breakfast cereal, they perked up.

'Where are we going today, Alan?' asked Kevin, scooping the last of the dark brown chocolate milk out of his bowl.

'My cave!' smiled Alan. 'Joshua's Cave.'

'Isn't it called Alan's Cave then?' asked Anna.

'No, unfortunately someone else found it first!' Alan winked. 'But it is a totally cool cave. You'll love it. So when you lot have finally finished eating, we can head off.'

'I'm done!' Kevin dropped his spoon into the bowl with a clatter.

'Mum, can I just have—?' began Tom, reaching towards the cereal packet.

'No,' said Mum firmly, whisking the packet off the table. 'You'll explode if you eat any more.

Come on, a quick wash and then out.'

Kevin and Tom raced to get ready in the bedroom they were sharing. They looked out at the blazing sunshine.

'What should we wear, d'you think?' asked Kevin. 'It's lovely out, but caves are dead cold, aren't they? Do we need jeans?' He rummaged through his case and pulled a pair out.

'Nah, I'm wearing shorts,' replied Tom. 'I'm tough. I'll take my new sweatshirt though.'

'OK, if you're going to freeze to death in a cave, then I'd better keep you company I suppose,' said Kevin, shoving the jeans back in and digging out his Ireland football shorts.

'Hey, good idea, I'll wear my Ireland ones too,' said Tom. He hunted through his neatly packed clothes. Soon they were all in a tangled heap. 'Oh no, don't say Mum didn't pack them! Mum!' he bellowed, and charged off to find her.

Eventually they were all ready. Tom's shorts had at last appeared in the very bottom of Anna's case. Mum discovered she hadn't packed any socks for herself, Anna and Tom, but Kevin and Alan had plenty of spare pairs to share.

'Honestly,' sighed Mum. 'How could I be so

daft? I wonder what else I've forgotten!'

'Nothing important, I'm sure,' Alan reassured her. 'Now, can we please set off?'

They clambered into Alan's huge hire car, a Ford SUV. They'd been too tired the previous day to take much notice of it. This time, though, they admired all the gizmos like the air conditioning and the built-in CD player.

'Listen to this!' said Alan, starting the engine before he'd put his seatbelt on.

'You have not fastened your seatbelt,' cautioned an invisible American woman.

'Wow! Does she say anything else?' Kevin was impressed.

'She tells you if you leave the lights on when you turn the engine off,' said Alan. 'That's all I've discovered so far.'

'And what's this?' asked Mum, looking at a small computer-like machine sitting on the dashboard.

'It's a Speaking Streetguide,' Alan informed her, turning it on so the coloured screen lit up.

'I'm none the wiser,' shrugged Mum.

'I know!' cried Tom. 'It's a GPS, isn't it.'

'Spot on!' smiled Alan.

'And even I know what GPS stands for,' said Kevin proudly. 'Global Positioning System. It uses satellites to show you where you are, doesn't it? Mrs D, we'll never get lost again!'

'Glad to hear it,' said Mum. 'We spend a lot of time getting lost when I'm driving. So, Alan, how exactly does this thing work?'

'It picks up the signals from satellites so it can lock onto your exact location. It shows where you are on a map. This system even directs you to where you want to go. Let's see, we're heading to Joshua's Cave from here . . .'. Alan punched a few instructions into the tiny keyboard. The boys watched, fascinated. 'OK, off we go.' He drove a few blocks towards the freeway. The little red dot that represented them moved a tiny way on the map. 'This thing is accurate to within a few feet.'

'Deadly,' observed Tom.

'But how does it show you where to go?' asked Kevin. 'The dot just shows where you are now, right?'

'Turn left onto the Johnson Freeway for four miles,' a tinny voice drawled.

'What was that?' gasped Kevin.

'The GPS!' laughed Alan. 'It talks!'

'Amazing,' said Mum. 'And I bet it doesn't get all huffy if you take a wrong turn and start having an argument with you, does it?'

'No, thank goodness,' replied Alan. 'But hey, the traffic's busy. I thought it would be quiet mid-morning.' He was right. The four lanes of the freeway were all bumper to bumper. 'Let's see if we can find another route.'

He typed in a few more instructions. The GPS immediately began to talk again, the tinny voice telling him to take the next exit from the freeway and head west.

'Just in time,' said Alan, quickly switching lanes to take the turning. 'I've never been this way before.'

It was an interesting journey along quiet roads. They passed through the sprawling suburbs of St Denis, and then suddenly they were in the countryside. Huge fields of corn spread to either side. They drove through long straggling villages that clung to the side of the road. They dipped in and out of the edge of a forest.

'People say there are bears in that forest,' remarked Alan.

'Oh!' squeaked Anna. 'I love bears. Can we go

and see them?'

'These aren't cuddly teddy bears, love,' Mum told her. 'These are big wild bears. Not the sort you'd have a picnic with!'

'No, they'd probably make a picnic out of you,' said Tom.

Anna shuddered and shrank back in her seat. 'Don't worry,' smiled Mum. 'We're safe in the car.'

'Yep, the good old GPS will keep us well away from bears,' added Alan. 'There's a special bear detection button just here.' Alan pretended to press one of the keys. 'Good, no bears today.'

Anna looked a lot happier. Alan winked at Kevin.

The scenery began to change, with some large hills becoming visible in the distance. There were expanses of bare rock amidst the general lushness of the countryside.

'Is that sandstone?' asked Mum.

'No, this is a limestone region, like the Burren, in Ireland, only larger. That explains why there are so many caves in Missouri. It's known as the Cave State, you know. It has more than 6,000 caves. Speleologist's heaven!' sighed Alan.

'Are you going to see all the caves while you're here, Alan?' asked Anna.

'I'm afraid not,' sighed Alan. 'Even if I managed to visit two caves every single day, it would still take me more than eight years to get round them all! I'm only here for six months. I'm doing some very detailed research on Joshua's Cave, but I have been off to see some of the others in my spare time. I'm hoping we can take several in while you're here.'

'That sounds good,' nodded Tom. 'I don't think I could ever get tired of visiting caves.'

'That's the spirit,' smiled Alan. 'Each cave is so fascinating, so amazingly unique—'

'Turn right at next intersection,' butted in the GPS.

'Wow, that made me jump!' admitted Kevin. 'I'd forgotten about our old navigator friend.'

'Oh look, the cave is signposted now,' observed Mum, as they drove past a huge, brightly painted billboard. 'Only five miles.'

'Great, I can't wait to see it,' said Tom.

'You won't be disappointed,' promised Alan.

And they weren't, even though they had to queue for half an hour to get in. Alan wanted to take them on the full touristy visit. The cave was enormous, far bigger than anything either Tom or Kevin had ever imagined. There was one huge cavern that was as big as a seven-storey building. And the whole cave was expertly lit, accentuating all the natural beauty of the various formations. The guide who took them round was very enthusiastic. She told them how the cave chronicled 400 million years of history, from its formation under the Silurian Sea that covered most of Northern America, through six ice ages, several huge earthquakes and various human exploits. At one time, the guide went on, saltpeter was extracted from the caves for use in gunpowder, and in later years, Jesse James, the famous bandit, used the cave as a hideout, as did escaping slaves.

Tom's head was reeling at all this, but he managed to think of a question when the guide paused for breath. 'How was the cave discovered?' he asked.

'By accident,' the guide replied. 'Some men were working in the fields above where we are now, and they stopped for a lunch break. They were kinda bored too, so when they saw an animal hole they began throwing rocks into it. Well, Joshua Greycroft rolled a real big rock into it, and it disappeared with a "thunk". So the guys decided to take a look and dug a larger hole into what is now the "old entrance" to the cave. We'll see that later on as part of the tour.'

'How cruel to throw rocks in an animal hole,' protested Anna.

'Yes, but look what was found as a result,' replied Tom. 'Besides, the animal, whatever it was, would have burrowed away safely, I bet.'

Anna looked satisfied.

The guide told everyone to follow her.

'Which bit of the cave do you work in?' Tom asked Alan, as they walked along. 'Not in this main part, surely?'

'No, there are several other private entrances to the cave,' said Alan. 'We go down an awful lot further into the cave network. There are some very unusual formations down there that we can't quite suss out just yet, but I'm starting to get some ideas about how they happened. There is still lots more checking out to do.' He looked around the huge cavern. 'Crikey! This is the first time I've seen this bit of the cave. It's amazing.'

'Will we be able to see where you're working, Alan?' asked Kevin.

'Probably not, I'm afraid. It's very tricky to get down there, plus it's all top secret stuff too. However, there's one area I will take you to sometime where we can see some fish and insects.'

'You don't get fish, surely?' exclaimed Mum. 'I'd have thought nothing could live down here.'

'Loads of creatures live in the caves,' said Alan. 'Near the entrances, you get minnows and catfish in the streams, and further in you get the real cave fish. They're peculiar small, white things. They're what we call troglobitic, which means they haven't got eyes.'

'How do they see then?' demanded Anna.

'They don't,' shrugged Alan. 'They don't need to. It's too dark to see anyway, deep down in the caves. You also get worms, snails, crayfish, spiders, and lots of tiny critters called pods.'

'Are they trollo . . . triblo . . . you know, blind?' asked Kevin.

'Some are, some aren't,' replied Alan. 'But shhh, the guide's about to talk again.'

5. Stormchasing

'Look at that sky!' said Mum, next morning over breakfast. 'It's going to bucket down.'

It certainly looked like it. The sky was an angry purply–grey colour. Tom thought it looked as though it wanted to squash them all.

'No cycling today then?' asked Kevin, disappointed.

'I don't think so,' said Mum, shaking her head. 'Looks like an indoors day today. How about shopping?'

'Great!' said Anna. She wanted to start buying presents for her friends at home.

Tom and Kevin exchanged glances. Trailing around endless shops didn't sound like a whole lot of fun today, not when there were more caves to visit. They tried to catch Alan's eye in the hope he might come up with an alternative activity for them, but he was buried in one of the many supplements that had come with the morning paper. Tom couldn't believe how big the daily papers were and how many sections they had. Surely no one could possibly read the whole thing in one day. It would take a week!

'Come on, let's get ready and hit the mall,' said Mum brightly. The boys didn't move. 'I bet there'll be a McDonald's . . .' she added sneakily, '. . . or a Wendy's.' That caught Kevin's attention.

'Maybe shopping *will* be fun,' he shrugged. Tom scowled at him.

Just then the phone rang. Alan dragged himself away from his paper and hurried into the hallway. The boys helped load the dishwasher, then began to slouch towards the bathroom to get washed. Suddenly Alan bounced back into the room.

'Cancel the shopping trip!' he beamed. 'We're going stormchasing!'

'What?' exclaimed Mum.

'Stormchasing. We're off chasing tornadoes – twisters! One of my friends at the university is a stormchaser in his spare time. He talks about it all the time, and it sounds fascinating. He promised he'd call me the next time conditions looked hopeful for twisters.' Alan was jumping around with excitement. 'I said you guys were here too and would love to come, and he said no problem.

He's got a large van and can fit us all in. He'll be here in about ten minutes!'

Tom and Kevin looked at each other again. Talk about brilliant! But would Mum let them go? Chasing twisters sounded pretty dangerous.

However, Mum looked thrilled. 'Fantastic! I've seen programmes about stormchasing on telly. It looks amazing. Quick boys, don't hang around!'

They were ready and waiting when a large, slightly battered Chevrolet Astro van drew up outside the apartment block. It was bristling with aerials, all different lengths and thicknesses. An incredibly large man stepped out and waved cheerily to them. He towered over Mum as he shook her hand and introduced himself as Chuck Foley, and then he scooped Anna off the ground for a hug as easily as though she were a doll.

'Wow, I've never seen such a tall fat guy!' whispered Kevin to Tom in amazement. Unfortunately he didn't whisper very quietly. Mum glared at Kevin, but Chuck burst out laughing.

'There's plenty of tall fat guys in the States, young fella,' he grinned. 'And compared to most of them, I'm small and skinny.' He laughed again and tipped Kevin's baseball hat over his eyes. He winked at Tom.

'Let's move,' he said. 'There's a beautiful storm brewing out there. I don't wanna miss any twisters.'

They climbed into the Chevrolet, marvelling at the array of equipment in it. They all recognised the GPS perched on the dashboard, but unlike Alan's, this was linked up to a laptop computer. The computer was also hooked up to a mobile phone. There was a small colour TV and even a tiny satellite dish inside the van. There were plenty of other electronic gizmos for who knew what purpose.

'Wow! This is class!' said Kevin admiringly. 'What's all the stuff for?'

'To help me find twisters,' laughed Chuck. 'I run weather analysis data on my computer all the time, together with the GPS program. I use the TV to keep half an eye on news and weather reports once the bad weather gets under way. The satellite dish picks up various specialised weather channels. My camcorder is hooked up to the TV too. I use a radio scanner to listen into SkyWarn weather reports, and I've got a CB radio so I can keep in touch with the other chasers out there. Oh yeah, I've got a ham radio too for reporting into the SkyWarn crew too. What else? Well . . . let's see, a printer, a camera mount, and most importantly, a cool box for drinks and snacks.'

'Most important!' agreed Kevin.

'You'll see what all the stuff does during the trip. So, settle down folks, and let's get going. I've been following this weather system for a few days now,' Chuck explained as he started the engine of his van and joined the stream of traffic. 'Good forecasting is real important. Today's what we call an active day. It's got the right combo of moisture, instability, lift and wind shear – that's everything we need for a supercell which can develop into a twister. A supercell is a long-lasting, rotating thunderstorm.'

'What are all those other things you said?' asked Tom. 'Eh, moisture, instability . . . and . . . and . . .'

'Lift and wind shear,' Chuck finished for him. 'OK, to keep it simple, well, moisture is easy enough to understand. Instability is when chunks of air are moving around all over the place. Lift is about getting the moist air up high so it condenses and turns into rain and hail. Wind shear is the last thing we need. That's where there's a change in wind speed and direction the higher you go.' He saw Tom's puzzled face. 'OK, imagine that at the surface the wind is blowing out of the east at 20km per hour. Go up 1,000m and it's blowing out of the southwest at 40km per hour, while up at 5,000m it's blowing out of the west at 50km per hour. That kinda set-up gets the rotation going.'

The CB radio crackled into life. Chuck picked it up and chatted away into it. The boys couldn't make out much of what he said. There were a lot of technical words and details, like 'dryline', 'storm evolution' and 'upper air soundings'. Tom caught Kevin's eye and shrugged.

'My ole buddy Chris Martin is out there,' said Chuck at last. 'He's been tracking all the data like I have and he thinks there's a real good chance that today won't be a bust.'

'A bust? What's that?' asked Mum.

'A bust is where you don't get a twister,' Chuck informed her. 'Some folks get real down when all their chasing comes to nothing, but I always enjoy myself. It's great just to be out and about, seeing the scenery and the dramatic weather.

Boy, have I seen some cool lightning shows!'

'I hope we see a twister,' said Kevin.

'Me too,' agreed Tom. 'But only if no one gets hurt by it,' he added, after a pause.

'You've hit the nail on the head, young fella,' nodded Chuck. 'Stormchasers who whoop and holler too much when they see a twister cause a lot of bad feeling. They forget that someone's on the receiving end of all that air rage. I'd prefer not to see a twister at all if there's any danger that it'll hurt people.'

'I hope we see a nice little twister far away from anywhere,' announced Anna.

'That would be just swell, honey,' agreed Chuck.

'How often do you go stormchasing, Chuck?' asked Mum.

'As often as I can during tornado season,' admitted the big man. 'Here in Tornado Alley the season runs from late April through to June. That's when the weather conditions are just about right for them. I don't show up for work a whole lot then.' He turned and winked at the children.

'Tornado Alley! I like that name,' said Tom.

'Tornado Alley runs pretty much straight up

the middle of the country, from Texas up to North Dakota and Minnesota, and into Canada,' explained Chuck. 'It's just a fancy name for the area where dangerous tornadoes are most likely to occur.'

'Mum, have there ever been any twisters in Ireland?' asked Tom.

'I have no idea,' confessed Mum. 'We'll have to do some research when we get back home.'

'We get some little ones in England every now and again,' said Alan.

Alan began to ask Chuck some detailed questions about tornadoes. Tom listened avidly but Kevin's concentration wandered. He gazed out of the side window at the tall piles of clouds in the sky and at the empty landscape stretching to either side. He swivelled in his seat and looked out of the back window. Not far behind he could see another vehicle, and that one seemed to have a lot of aeriels too. It was bright pink all over!

'Chuck, I think there's another stormchaser behind us!' he said.

Chuck glanced up into his rearview mirror.

'Sure thing! That there's the Pink Elephant, darnedest chasemobile I ever came across. That's my old buddy Chris Martin. He's the guy I told you about earlier. I'll give him a shout on the CB.' Chuck picked up his radio receiver and began to speak into it. 'Mister Twister calling Pink Elephant, over.'

He began chatting away over the radio to his friend. After a fairly long chat, he signed off.

'Good news!' he said. 'Chris thinks we've got a good chance of something exciting round here real soon. Excuse me for a while, I need to check out some new data.'

Chuck told Alan to press some keys on the computer keyboard, and some weather data popped up. Alan relayed to Chuck what it said. Chuck looked pleased. Next he used his ham radio to pick up the latest SkyWarn information.

'We're spot on for some action,' he grinned happily. Then he glanced at his watch.

'Hey, anyone fancy a quick bite of lunch? By the looks of it we've got a bit of time before things really start to develop. But I'm warning you, don't drink too much! When we start chasing in earnest, there'll be no chance to stop for comfort breaks! There's a service station coming right up. We'll take a break, OK?'

'Totally OK!' nodded Kevin.

6. Twister

After three-quarters of an hour, and very little coke, they were back on the road. This time there was a lot less chatting. Chuck stationed Alan by the computer, telling him to shout out when he saw certain strings of data appearing. Tom and Kevin were on 'visuals', watching out of the windows. Mum was in charge of the video camera and Anna was to keep everyone supplied with candy to keep them alert.

The sky was a deep greeny black, with huge towering grey clouds in it. The Pink Elephant, which was travelling in front of them now, stuck out vividly against the darkness. Suddenly the rain began to lash down, smacking against the windscreen of the Astro in huge splotches. The noise was incredible, but within seconds it became louder still, as the rain turned to hail. But this wasn't hail like Tom and Kevin occasionally saw in Ireland. These hailstones were easily the size of golfballs! They crashed down onto the van relentlessly.

'Good heavens!' cried Mum. 'I've never seen hailstones this big before.'

'They're big, but they ain't huge,' said Chuck. 'I've had icy tennis balls bouncing off me.'

'Will the windscreen hold?' asked Alan, wincing as the hailstones crunched down.

'Should do, it's special toughened glass, but you never know for sure,' shrugged Chuck. 'I get through several windscreens a year. I tell you, it's an expensive hobby all right.'

'Hey, lightning,' called Tom, as a huge fork of light shot through the sky and speared the earth.

'Great!' cried Chuck. 'Keep watching. Any time now we should see a twister touch down.'

Tom could hardly keep still, he was so excited. And scared as well. Over lunch, Chuck had told them several times that there was no way they'd be in danger, but Tom was still nervous. He was especially surprised that Mum seemed so cool about it all. Usually she was the one who worried about everything. Tom glanced at Kevin. He was twisting around on his seat, scanning in every direction so as not to miss any tornado that might appear. He didn't look at all jittery. 'Why am I being such a wimp?' Tom asked himself crossly.

Alan caught sight of the worried expression.

'Anyone else shaking in their shoes?' Alan enquired. 'I'm feeling pretty tense.'

Tom felt better at once. If a grown-up was nervous too, well then, it was all right for him to feel that way.

Alan smiled to himself and glanced back at the computer screen. 'I think we've got something here,' he told Chuck excitedly.

'And I've got something too!' cried Kevin, pointing out of his window. 'There's a triangle-type thing coming down out of the sky.'

'Where?' shouted everyone at once, craning their necks to look.

'That's it all right!' declared Chuck. 'That's our twister. Down she comes!'

They watched in awe as the distant cone of dark swirling air spiralled down to the ground.

'Touchdown,' nodded Chuck. He picked up his radio receiver and spoke hurriedly into it, keeping one eye on the road in front of him, and one eye firmly on the twister.

'This looks like an F0 or F1 twister to me – nothing too drastic, although it'll do some damage,' Chuck told them, following the Pink

Elephant off the highway onto a side road so as to get a better view of the tornado.

'What's the F for?' asked Kevin.

'Fujita,' Chuck told him. 'Tornadoes are measured on the Fujita scale. It measures their intensity – that's to say, not how tall they are or how wide they are, but how *mean* they are! It's all about the amount of damage they do. Guys like me, when we're out chasing, we like to guess the intensity of the twister we're tracking. We look at how fast it's turning, and how much debris it's chucking around. But it's not till after the twister has passed by that you get the official estimate. The National Weather Service sends its guys out to give it an F-scale rating. Sometimes they call in insurance engineers to help.'

'What do they base their judgement on?' Mum wanted to know.

'Stuff like: Are any walls still standing? Have roofs been blown off? That kinda thing,' explained Chuck. 'It's not a foolproof method of sizing up a tornado. It depends a lot on who's doing the looking. I mean, someone who hasn't seen many twisters might see a bit of damage and think, "Gee whizz, that must have been an F5." That happens a lot with journalists. They usually make out things are a whole lot worse than they really are. They see trees that have been levelled, but don't take into account that they're shallow rooted and standing in soft ground, so they were real easy to topple. And OK, a roof's been blown half a mile down the road, but it was only attached with a few nails and caught the air like a sail.'

'What's the strongest twister – an F10?' hazarded Tom.

'No, the Fujita scale goes from 0 to 6, but an F6 is what we call an inconceivable tornado. You just can't imagine what one of those would be like. An F5 is as bad as you ever need to get. That's known as an incredible tornado. It does stuff like lift whole houses up, chuck cars and lorries well over a hundred metres and mess up reinforced concrete structures real bad. Even the lowest intensity tornado, an F0, brings chimneys and trees down. All twisters are nasty, especially if you're in their path.'

'Have you ever seen an F5?' asked Tom.

'Yes sir,' nodded Chuck. 'I nearly came to a sticky end in one of those. I almost let it get too close to me. But I'll tell you about that another time. Hey, this baby's changing direction, look!'

The twister suddenly veered to the left.

'It's coming towards us!' squeaked Anna.

'Kinda looks that way,' grinned Chuck. 'Don't worry. Look on my computer there, you'll see it's heading well away from us. Isn't that right Alan?' Alan, who'd been monitoring the screen carefully, nodded firmly. 'I'm taking no risks with you guys on board,' Chuck went on. 'Mind you, I don't ever take risks. Stormchasing is a bit of a misleading name. What we do is really just stormwatching or stormavoiding!'

'Not as catchy,' observed Tom.

'That's true. Hey, I'll pull in here,' said Chuck, seeing a layby. 'We'll watch it go by.'

'The Pink Elephant isn't stopping,' pointed out Kevin, disappointed. He didn't want to stop. He wanted to carry on stormchasing.

Mum pulled a 'shh' face at Kevin.

'We're quite close enough here,' said Chuck. 'Anyway, this baby's running out of gas.'

'What! The van?' gasped Tom. How would they get home?

'No!' laughed Chuck. 'The twister. She's getting blurry round the edges and slowing down.'

'Why is it a girl?' demanded Anna. 'Don't you get boy twisters?'

Chuck chuckled. 'It's just a habit we chasers have of turning the twisters into people.'

'They do that with hurricanes, don't they?' said Tom, keen to show off his knowledge. 'At one time, they were always given a girl's name, but I think women got cross about that, so they started using boys' names too. Do twisters have names, like hurricanes do?'

'We usually call them after the place they touch down, but only if they're significant,' Chuck explained. He looked back to the twister and then sighed. 'There, she's . . . sorry, it's gone. But the main thing is no one got hurt by it.'

'Good,' said Anna, pleased.

They stood staring for quite a while at where the twister had been.

'I guess we'll head for home now,' said Chuck, at last. 'I need to analyse all my data tonight, and update my files.' Suddenly Kevin yawned, long and loud. Chuck leaned back and poked him good naturedly in the tummy. 'And you guys look all tuckered out. You need some rest. But hey, was that swell or what?'

7. More Storms

The next day didn't start well. They were all grumpy, knowing that today couldn't possibly match the excitement of yesterday. Whatever they ended up doing, it was going to be an anticlimax. And Mum had a rotten headache.

'It's this weather,' she muttered, looking up at the rain-filled skies. 'It's very heavy and hot.'

Just as they were starting to liven up a little after breakfast and beginning to make plans for the day, Alan got a phone call. But today it wasn't the offer of stormchasing. There was a problem with a computer program Alan had set up to analyse some rock samples he had taken from Joshua's Cave. Apparently the cleaner had dusted the computer keyboard while the program was running and messed things up. Alan was furious as he left the apartment.

'It took me hours to set up,' he moaned, giving Mum a quick kiss on the cheek. 'I'll try and get back for lunchtime.'

'OK,' sighed Mum, disappointed that Alan

was having to go to work.

'So what'll we do?' asked Tom. 'There's loads of stuff on the telly we could watch.' He and Kevin were determined to work their way through all the hundreds of channels on American television.

Mum shot him a cross look. 'Do you honestly think we came all the way from Ireland to America just to watch TV?'

There was obviously only one answer to that.

'No, of course not,' piped up Kevin. 'Tom, what dumb ideas you have.'

Tom shrugged. Mum managed a weak smile. 'Come on,' she said. 'We'll walk into town and check out a museum.'

But walking into town was easier said than done. They set off along the pavement in the right direction, only to find that it suddenly stopped at the edge of a busy road and there was no way of getting across it.

'Surely there's a subway or a footbrige,' yelled Mum above the din of the traffic.

'I don't see anything,' Tom yelled back.

'Maybe there's something further along,' suggested Kevin loudly.

They picked their way through the parking lot on their right, but that just ended in a barrier.

'What a crazy country, when you can't even walk places,' fumed Mum.

They ended up going back home and calling a taxi. The driver looked amazed when Mum told him how they'd tried to walk into town.

'Walk?' he echoed in horror. 'Say, folks don't walk into town round here. They ride.'

Mum looked exasperated. Tom knew exactly what she was thinking. She was thinking how bad for the environment it was for everyone to drive everywhere, and how unhealthy.

The taxi dropped them outside the dog museum. Anna whooped with joy when she saw it. Even the boys cheered up a bit. Everything started off well. There were photos and models of famous dogs, and huge boards telling their stories. But when they came across one heroic dog who had been stuffed to preserve him, Anna freaked. She began to cry and although Mum pleaded, she wouldn't stop. A museum warden icily asked them to leave at once. Mum dragged Anna out.

'For goodness sake!' she exploded when they got outside and Anna calmed down at last.

'Thanks to you we've been thrown out of a museum.' She looked daggers at Anna who started to sob. But suddenly Kevin started giggling.

'Mrs D, we'll probably be banned from all the museums in St Denis now!' he grinned.

Tom, who'd been desperately trying to keep a straight face, began to laugh too. Kevin guffawed noisily. Anna stopped snivelling and started laughing squeakily. Mum tried to ignore them and carry on being cross, but she couldn't. She smiled.

'OK, you win,' she laughed. 'That poor old dog was a bit gross, wasn't he. But please, no more tantrums, Annie.'

They popped into a diner and bought some coffee for Mum, and fizzy drinks and muffins for the others. They browsed half-heartedly in a few shops, then flagged a taxi down and went home for lunch. They all hoped Alan would get back soon so they could do something nice together in the afternoon.

At last, at about half past one, he burst through the door. He was beaming from ear to ear.

'Now, do you want the bad news or the good news!' he asked cheerfully.

'Well, the bad news can't be that bad, judging

from your grin,' smiled Mum, 'so let's have that.'

'Actually, it's not great,' admitted Alan, looking more serious, 'it's just that the good news is so much better. The bad news is that I'll have to pop back to the department for a bit longer to carry on fixing the computer.'

Mum's face fell.

'But wait till you hear the good news,' Alan went on. 'I've just been offered a permanent job. Here, in America! Apparently some extra funding has just come through, and the department head is so impressed with the work I've been doing, and values it so highly, he came straight over to see me and make the offer. What d'you think?'

No one said anything. They just stared at him.

'Well?' Alan prompted.

'A permanent job? Here?' Mum sat down. She looked white with shock.

'It's everything I've been looking for,' enthused Alan. 'Complete freedom in the research I do, excellent resources, loads of funding and I'll be very well paid. It's a once-in-a-lifetime opportunity for me – for all of us. I'd – *we'd* be really happy here in the States, I know we would.'

'What, you'd all come and live here?' said

Kevin, stricken. 'But Tom, you're my best friend in the whole world. I'll hardly ever get to see you.' To everyone's horror, he burst into tears and ran out of the room. That was such an unKevinish thing to do, no one knew how to react.

'Oh, look what you've done,' snapped Mum. 'For goodness' sake, Alan, you might have talked to me about this first in private. Tom, Anna, go and find Kevin, and put the telly on.'

'But Mum, you said we didn't come all this way to—' Tom reminded her.

'Put the telly on,' ordered Mum in her dangerous voice. Tom knew better than to argue this time. He and Anna hurried out of the room. They found Kevin curled up on his bed hugging his favourite Manchester United scarf.

'Hey, cheer up dude,' said Tom, sitting on the bed beside him.

'Please don't leave Ireland,' begged Kevin. 'I won't have any friends if you do.'

'Rubbish! You've got loads of friends at school. Aidan, Liam, Oliver, John . . .' Tom began to reel off a list of names. It was true, everyone liked Kevin.

'But they're not real friends, not like you,'

cried Kevin.

'Thanks, buddy,' said Tom. 'You're my world's best ever friend too.' He fell silent.

Anna watched the two boys with big confused eyes. Then she winced as she heard Mum and Alan shouting. Tom walked over and gave her a hug. Anna clung tightly to him.

'Doesn't look like we'll be living here with Alan anyway,' Tom said over his shoulder to Kevin ruefully. 'Not after a fight like this!'

'It's just a row,' Kevin told him, sitting up and sniffing. 'Mum and Dad row all the time.'

'No they don't,' protested Tom. 'I've never ever heard your mum and dad shout at each other.'

'They don't do it when other people are around,' Kevin said. 'OK, and they don't do it all the time, but they do have some shouting matches. Poor Mum gets so sick of being stuck in her wheelchair sometimes, and Dad feels all helpless – they get cross at each other. It's just shouting, it clears the air. They're still nuts about each other. Like your mum and Alan.'

'I don't know,' said Tom doubtfully. Mum sounded really angry. 'They don't sound very nuts about each other just now.'

A door slammed. Tom and Anna sprang apart,

and Kevin leapt out of bed as Mum stormed in.

'Kids, we're going out!' she snapped.

They hurried to the door. Mum grabbed Alan's car keys off the hall table.

'He can get the taxi this time,' Mum frowned, seeing Tom looking at her in astonishment.

She hustled them into the car. Tom looked out anxiously, waiting for Alan to come rushing after them and tell them to get out of his car. But he needn't have worried, Alan was tied up with another urgent phone call about yet more problems with his computer program.

Mum started the engine and tried to drive off. But she couldn't get the gearstick out of the parking position.

'What's wrong with this wretched car!' she cursed.

'Er, I think you have to press down on the brake pedal,' said Tom. He'd been watching Alan.

Mum snorted. 'Stupid automatic cars.' But she followed Tom's suggestion and they began to lurch forwards. They kangarooed awkwardly out onto the freeway. The children didn't dare make any remarks. Luckily, though, Mum soon got the hang of driving without gears.

They drove for quite a long while, and a lot

faster than Mum usually drove. She grumbled under her breath from time to time and looked very tense. The three children kept a low profile in the back. But eventually Kevin couldn't help piping up with 'Where are we going, Mrs D?'

That brought Mum back to normal.

'Crikey, I've no idea,' she admitted, slowing down dramatically. 'Oh kids, I'm so sorry. I was so mad. I . . . I . . . oh, never mind.' She looked around at the wide open plains around them. 'Actually I do know where we are. We're lost!'

'My favourite place!' grinned Kevin.

'We're not lost, not with the GPS,' Tom reminded them. He clambered into the front seat next to Mum.

'A back-seat passenger has unfastened a seatbelt. Your front-seat passenger has not fastened the seatbelt,' announced the car's safety device, instantly alerted by Tom's antics. Clearly there were sensors under every seat.

'Get a seatbelt on quick, young man,' warned Mum. 'I don't want this thing nagging me!'

Tom clicked his seatbelt on. 'Now, let's have a look,' said Tom inspecting the GPS. 'It can't be that hard to suss out, surely.' He tentatively pressed a few buttons. Nothing happened. Tom looked puzzled.

'Go on Einstein, you'll figure it out,' Kevin encouraged him.

As Tom concentrated on the task, Kevin looked out of the car windows. There was a steady stream of traffic on the other carriageway of the freeway, tearing by in the opposite direction. Kevin glanced behind. That was weird, they had this carriageway to themselves. The sky was really black and rain had started to lash down.

'It's just like Ireland!' he remarked. Then a thought hit him. 'It's just like yesterday too. Before the twister.'

'I was beginning to think that as well,' agreed Mum cautiously. 'Any luck, Tom? I'm beginning to think we'd better head for home.'

'I've found a menu here,' said Tom, as one popped up on the GPS's screen. 'Now which command do we need? 'Find' maybe?'

'Don't worry,' smiled Mum. 'I can see a roadsign ahead. What does it say? Oh, Roytown. Never heard of that.'

'I have,' Anna piped up.

The others all turned to look at her.

'How come?' demanded Tom.

'It was on the telly this morning when I was watching with Alan,' said Anna. 'It was on that bit they have about the weather.'

'The weather forecast?' suggested Mum.

'Sort of,' replied Anna. 'But more the bit where they tell you where you might get tornadoes.'

'A bad weather warning!' cried Mum.

'That's it,' nodded Anna.

Mum pulled off the road and screeched to a halt. 'No wonder everyone else is going the other way. Right, we need to look for a turn.'

Mum set off again at top speed. Tom desperately juggled with the GPS.

'Got something!' he shouted at last, as a map popped up onto the screen. 'And I've pinpointed where we are. Let's zoom in a bit more. Uh oh, no turn-offs for ages.'

'What!' exclaimed Mum. 'And I can't do a U-turn onto the other carriageway. There's a crash barrier in the way.'

'Can't you just drive back along this carriageway, you know, the wrong way?' suggested Kevin. 'There's no one else on it.'

'Kevin Murphy, you're a genius!' cried Mum.

'Let's just hope we don't meet any cops though.'

Kevin looked very pleased with himself.

'Tom, see if you can find us a quick way home,' said Mum as she did a neat U-turn and began heading back the way they'd just come, but staying in the hard shoulder for safety. 'Kevin and Anna, keep your eyes peeled for tornadoes touching down. I'll watch out for cops!'

The rain was heavier now. It smashed onto the tarmac and bounced back up. Mum had the car windscreen wipers on at full pelt but she could still hardly see. Then suddenly the rain eased for a moment.

'That's better,' smiled Mum, feeling relieved. It looked like they were getting away from the worst weather now. But next second her spirits plummeted as hail began to hurl itself at them. The hailstones weren't as big as the ones they'd seen yesterday, but they were big enough. Mum cringed as they ricocheted off the windscreen with sickening thuds.

Tom had been playing around with the GPS. He was beginning to make sense of it now, but he couldn't find the command that made it speak directions. 'Mum, we can't go too far wrong if we just keep heading down this road for now. It takes us more or less straight back to St Denis. We'll have to cut back onto the proper carriageway somewhere or other though, because we need a right turn after about twelve kilometres.'

'OK,' Mum nodded.

'Hey, wow, look at that!' yelled Kevin suddenly, making them all jump. 'There's a twister coming down. And boy, it's enormous!'

'Where is it?' Mum wanted to know.

'Kind of left and behind us.'

'How far?'

Kevin had to admit defeat here. 'I don't really know, but it looks quite a way off.'

Tom left his GPS station and looked out of the side window. The huge whirling mass of darkness was swooping down from the sky. Kevin was right, it was hard to tell exactly where it was. But it did seem to be moving away from them.

'I think we're OK, Mum,' he sighed with relief. 'Looks like it's heading to Roytown.'

'Well, thank goodness *we're* not.' Mum sighed with relief too, but she didn't slow down at all. 'Great, I can see a junction ahead. We'll be able to switch back to the proper side of the road at last.

All this law-breaking makes me nervous!'

A minor road cut across the highway and Mum nipped onto the southbound carriageway again. They all relaxed.

After a few moments, Tom felt brave enough to ask a question. 'Er Mum, are you still going to marry Alan?'

'I hope so,' said Mum softly. 'This living in America business needs some thinking about though. Especially in the middle of Tornado Alley! Look, don't any of you get upset about things. I'll sort it all out.' She smiled across at Tom and reached to give his hand a squeeze, but a sudden bellow from Kevin made her swerve and quickly grab the steering wheel with both hands again.

'The twister! It's coming after us now!'

'Are you sure?' Mum gasped.

'I'm sure! I'm sure!' cried Kevin.

Mum's mouth went dry and her hands clenched the steering wheel so tightly that her fingers went white. She pressed down even harder on the accelerator but the car didn't respond. They were already going flat out. And anyway, hadn't she learned from *Discovery Channel* that you can't outrun a tornado, and that being in a car during one is just about the worst place to be?

'How are we doing?' she asked.

'It's gaining on us, Mrs D.'

'Any turnings coming up Tom?' was her next question.

'Nope, afraid not. This road just goes on and on like a long line,' Tom told her.

'Cool!' said Kevin unexpectedly. 'There's lightning coming out of the tornado! Loads of it!' For a moment he'd forgotten their predicament.

'I'm sure I'd think it was awesome if it wasn't chasing us,' remarked Mum.

'Oh yeah, it is, isn't it? Not so cool,' Kevin corrected himself.

Mum could see the twister in her rearview mirror now. It had swung round so it was directly behind them. It was following them along the highway, throwing up the crash barriers and roadside trees with its deadly spinning.

'Mummy!' squeaked Anna. 'Will it get us?'

'No it won't,' Mum said firmly. 'I won't let it.'

She sounded so confident, Tom almost believed her. Anna clearly did. She sat back happily in her seat and started humming. Tom shot

Kevin a worried look. Kevin pulled a face back. Things didn't look good.

'Are there any bridges, Tom?' asked Mum suddenly. 'Maybe we could shelter under one.'

'No, no,' cried Kevin. 'I saw a film about a twister once, which was really good but a bit long, and someone in it, a sort of professor-type guy, was telling this other guy, who was an escaped prisoner, although you didn't know that till the end, not to hide under a bridge during a tornado!'

'There isn't a bridge anyway,' wailed Tom when Kevin had finished rambling on. 'There's nothing. There's just more road and some houses.'

'Houses!' echoed Mum. 'Where are they?'

'A bit further on. Well, I mean, I *think* they're houses,' confessed Tom. 'They're just black squares on the GPS. They could be grain stores or barns or, well, anything.'

'Whatever they are, they'll have to do,' said Mum grimly. 'We're not going to stay ahead of that thing much longer.' It completely filled her rearview mirror and they could hear it roaring.

'Go away, you stupid twister,' Kevin yelled.

'Nearly there,' said Tom, watching the red dot on the GPS that represented the car moving towards the black squares on the screen.

Mum joggled up and down in her seat, uselessly urging the car to go faster. 'I can't see anything yet,' she cried, peering through the windscreen.

Tom stared desperately at the GPS. Maybe he was completely misreading it? Maybe the squares were duck ponds or horse troughs. He looked up, willing a building to appear ahead of them. Beside them the solid crash barrier gave way to hedgerows. And there, suddenly, something loomed out of the gloom. He pointed.

'I see it, I see it,' shrieked Mum. It was a house and now they were nearly on it. 'Hold tight. I'm taking a shortcut.'

Without slowing down, Mum veered off the carriageway, blasted through the hedgerow and bounced over a rough field.

'Hey, Mrs D, you'd make a great rally driver!' Kevin grinned.

Mum managed a small smile as she fought the car to keep it under control over the rough terrain.

'Unscheduled detour from route!' the GPS suddenly complained, making them all jump.

'Oh shut up, dopey machine,' snapped Tom.

'Never mind about that,' said Mum. 'Tom, there's a torch in the glove compartment. Grab it. Now, the minute we stop, run for the house. Don't bother knocking, just go straight in. We need to get down into the basement or under the stairs.' But now that they were practically at the house, they realised that it was a ruin. It had no roof and no windows.

'What on earth good is that?' Mum exploded in panic. She looked behind them, although she really didn't need to. She knew just how close the twister was. The car was starting to shake.

'It's better than nothing, isn't it?' cried Tom.

That snapped Mum back to her senses. 'Yes, of course. There could still be a cellar. Hurry!'

She shoved Tom out of his door before leaping out and taking over from Kevin in dragging Anna off the back seat. They dashed through the empty doorway and looked around, urgently scanning for some sort of shelter.

'Look, look!' yelled Tom, barely making himself heard above the roaring twister that was bearing down on them. 'A trapdoor.' He pointed to a rusty iron ring on a square of wood, just showing through some weeds on the ground.

Mum grabbed hold of it, and heaved with all her might. It groaned but didn't move.

'I can't budge it,' she screamed.

'We'll help,' shouted Kevin, and he and Tom took hold of the ring too. The rusty metal cut into their hands but they didn't care. But still the trapdoor didn't open.

Mum's eyes filled with tears of fear and failure. She dashed them away angrily, but as she did so, she caught sight of a huge rusty bolt holding the trap door shut. No wonder it wouldn't open! She seized the bolt and dragged it back with all her might. It resisted at first, but then suddenly shot back, crushing her little finger. Mum barely registered the pain.

'Now pull again,' she ordered.

This time it creaked open. A steep, narrow, filthy concrete staircase led down into the festering gloom.

'In, quick,' snapped Mum.

They tumbled through the door into the darkness. Tom switched the torch on. Thank goodness they had it. Mum stretched up and swung the heavy trapdoor back over their heads. She was relieved to see a bolt on the inside too –

clearly this place had been used to shelter from tornadoes in the past. She began to slide the bolt home, but all at once the door began rattling up and down. The twister was almost on top of them. Mum heaved with all her might. She lifted her feet off the steps so that she was literally hanging from the door handle. For a second the trapdoor clunked heavily into place, but then it jumped back up. As it did, the roar of the tornado almost deafened her. And she yelped with pain as tiny shards of debris in the spiralling vortex speared her hands.

'It's not my day,' thought Mum grimly.

Then, for the first time in her life, Mum wished she weighed twice as much. That way she'd be able to drag the door shut. But of course, there was a much simpler way to gain weight.

'Boys!' she yelled. 'Grab hold of a leg each, and pull down as hard as you can.'

Tom hesitated in confusion, handing Anna the torch to hold. 'Eh, whose leg, Mum?'

'Mine!' screeched Mum above the twister's thundering roar. 'NOW!'

The boys clung onto Mum's slim legs and heaved. For an instant Mum honestly thought her arms might pop out of their sockets. But still she couldn't quite get the trapdoor to shut. Just as she was beginning to think she couldn't hold on any longer, Anna put the torch down and grabbed hold of Tom. The extra few kilograms did the trick. The door closed and Mum thrust the bolt into place.

'Well done, but please let go now, guys!' she gasped.

Her arms felt weak and trembly, and she could have collapsed in a heap, but Mum knew they weren't necessarily safe yet. She picked the torch up and flicked its beam around the cellar. In one corner there was an ancient mattress and some black and mouldy sacks.

'Quick, get under those!' she instructed. 'They should protect us from any falling debris.' Presumably that was what these things had done in the past in this long-abandoned tornado shelter.

They burrowed under the mattress and sacks. Tom half expected the mound to be already sheltering rats and mice and he wasn't looking forward to bumping into them. But there was nothing furry and squeaky waiting for them. Only an enormous quantity of spiders and other insects. Tom felt them crawling all over him. Normally he'd have freaked, but in the circumstances he just shuddered. They had far worse things than a few spiders to worry about.

Without needing to be told, they all held onto each other, and waited for the weather to do its worst. The old wooden trapdoor groaned and rattled louder and louder as the twister whirled above it, sucking at it with incredible energy. Anna buried her face deep into Mum's hair to stifle a scream. They all clung to each other, rigid with fear. Tom felt hot tears burning his eyes.

'Be brave!' he told himself angrily, but he couldn't. He was as scared now as he'd ever been in his life. He hoped and prayed that the trapdoor would hold. But suddenly, with a sickening, splintering sound, the middle panel of the door broke away and was sucked up into the air. The weirdest sensations followed. First it seemed like they were being pressed to the floor by a huge force.

'There's an elephant sitting on me!' grunted Kevin. But no sooner had he said that than the pressure eased. Now it felt like they were being dragged upwards. Tom knew this was to do with the air pressure changes between the rotating winds and the updraft in the centre of the tornado.

But that didn't make it any easier to deal with. He fought against it with all his might, pushing himself down into the ground.

The mattress above them struggled to take off. A few of the sacks were ripped away. Tom tried to shout 'Hang on!' but the air seemed to be sucked out of his lungs. He could only mouth the words.

How long the exhausting battle between the twister and the four of them raged, they didn't know. It could have been just a few seconds or several minutes. The time seemed to stretch on forever, to stand still, as they clung frantically to each other and their protective covering. Then, suddenly, it was over. The mattress slumped down on top of them again, causing a fresh wave of alarmed spiders to scuttle out over them. But they were too drained and shocked to notice. They continued to cower in their dusty hiding place.

8. A Shock for Alan

Alan paid the taxi driver and strode into the university with a face like thunder. He was mad because of having to come back to work, mad because of the row and mad because Jane had taken the car. He locked himself into his office, dumped his briefcase down angrily beside the computer that was causing all the trouble and resentfully set to work on it. His office was in the basement and had no windows. It was a dismal little box of a room, but it served its purpose. Muttering and mumbling, he checked through the endless lines of computer code that made up his analysis program.

By four o'clock he still hadn't located where the errors were occurring. He was totally fed up. He hated computers. Just at the moment he also hated caves, cleaners – and America. He hated everything, except Jane. He wanted to talk to her and sort this stupid business between them out.

He sighed, stretched, let himself out of his office and headed to the staff kitchen and common room on the ground floor. He was cross when he saw through the glass panel in the door that someone else was already there. He didn't need company just now, but he did need coffee.

'That's a real bad twister happened today,' observed Hal, a computer lecturer, as Alan came into the room. Hal was sipping coffee out of an enormous mug, feet on the coffee table and watching the small TV in the corner of the room.

'Where did it touch down?' asked Alan.

'About ten miles southeast of Roytown. Not usually a place that gets many twisters. Look, here comes another report about it now,' said Hal.

Alan fixed himself a much smaller mug of coffee than Hal's and perched next to his colleague on the sofa. A female news reporter was breathlessly and enthusiastically summing up all the damage the twister had done so far.

'Just look at this!' she exclaimed joyfully as the camera focussed in on a tree behind her. A car was tangled in its groaning branches.

'Wow!' Alan was horrified. 'That car is the same make as the one I've got. They're heavy, solid things.'

The camera zoomed in on the car. The number

plate was now clearly visible. Alan went white.

'Oh good grief,' he croaked, his mug of coffee tumbling from his shaking hand. 'That *is* my car.'

Hal looked at him in horror as the reporter chattered away happily about how no one knew what had happened to the car's occupants, but police were trying to track them down.

'Say, you're not kidding me?' asked Hal.

But Alan was already heading out of the door, stabbing madly at the number keys on his mobile phone. His fingers were trembling so much he kept punching in the wrong numbers.

'Stupid thing!' he shouted, hurling the phone at the floor. It skidded along the corridor and crashed into the wall, bits of plastic breaking off.

'Stay cool.' Hal had caught up with Alan. 'I'm sure your folks are OK. Look, what's their mobile number?' Hal flipped open his own phone. Alan took a deep breath and reeled off the number. Hal made the call, but there was no reply.

Alan was pacing up and down. 'What do I do? Call the police? Phone round hospitals? What?'

Hal thought for a moment. 'Where were they heading today?'

Alan groaned. 'I don't know. We had a blazing

row at lunchtime and Jane took off with the kids. Oh no, if anything's happened to her and the kids . . . and I don't get the chance to say "Sorry" . . .' Alan's voice trailed off. 'How could I be so stupid?' he wailed suddenly. 'It was a stupid argument, and all my fault.'

'Rows happen,' shrugged Hal. 'Look, why don't we give Chuck a buzz. He'll know where that twister hit. Maybe he can give you a ride that way. You know he loves chasing twisters.'

'That's brilliant,' nodded Alan. Hal was already dialling the number. He gave Alan a thumbs-up as someone answered. He had a short chat with Chuck, then snapped the phone shut.

'We've just caught him,' he told Alan. 'Chuck's just about to set off and look over the damage. He'll wait for you in the main car park.'

Alan launched himself towards the nearest staircase and raced down to the car park. As he burst out of the main doors of the building, he saw the Chevrolet Astro just pulling up. He tore the front door open and leapt in before the van had even stopped. Chuck glanced at Alan's white face, gave him a quick nod, then floored the accelerator and sped out of the car park onto the freeway.

Without being asked, Alan stationed himself by the computer to monitor the data that came in. He could see the twister, showing up as a bright red splodge in the top right hand quarter of the small map of Missouri. The rest of the screen showed graphs and series of figures, changing constantly as new data came onstream.

'It's a nasty one,' Chuck confirmed. 'I'd say we're looking at an F3, F4 maybe.'

Alan felt sick. How on earth could anyone survive that, caught out in the open? He also felt very guilty. Sitting on his desk at work were several copies of a pamphlet on tornado drill that he'd meant to give to Jane and the children so they would know what to do if they suddenly found themselves coping with an approaching twister. But he'd forgotten to bring them home. He clenched his fists angrily.

Chuck began calling up colleagues on his CB radio. Alan recognised the Pink Elephant call sign. He heard Chuck explaining about Jane and the children and asking Chris to keep an eye open.

'OK, what we'll do is start where this twister touched down and follow its path. You see the pale blue trace on the screen? That's what we need. Use the menu and zoom in on it, and call up a road map overlay. Then activate the GPS link and sing out the instructions it comes up with.'

Alan did as he was told, glad to be doing something positive at last. But his hands trembled as he typed. He, Jane and the children had been through some nasty scrapes in the past, but this had to be one of the worst.

The GPS had mapped a route by now so Alan relayed the directions to Chuck. It wasn't too long before they were on the trail of the twister. Alan was horrified by the devastation it had caused in the countryside – uprooted trees, strong wooden railings reduced to splinters, flattened barns.

'Are there many casualties?' he asked Chuck.

'I'm getting a few reports over the radio of injuries,' replied Chuck. 'Nothing too serious – so far. And the latest intel is that the twister is losing strength now.'

That was good news but it didn't do much to cheer him up. Jane and the children had been caught up in the worst of the twister. Alan groaned again. What had become of them?

9. Anna's Flowers

Is it safe to come out now?' came Kevin's very muffled voice. 'This lot stinks even worse than Tom's feet. I don't think I can stand it much longer!'

'And I'm sure there's a spider building a web up my nose,' added Tom, mournfully.

Mum cautiously loosened her vice-like grip on Anna and gently eased the pile of rotting sacks off her head. She wasn't sure how long it was since the tornado had passed over them. They'd all been too scared and shocked to move for a long time. But now it was definitely all calm. Birds were singing and a shaft of sunlight was filtering down through the broken trapdoor.

'All clear!' she sighed. They'd survived the twister's horror, but she was too drained to feel triumphant. And anyway, it had been more by good luck than good judgement. She was wracked with guilt at the thought of how she alone had placed them all in the path of this whirling vortex of destruction. She should never have driven off in a huff after her row with Alan. It was all her fault.

'Hey Mum, cheer up,' said Tom, seeing her distraught face. 'Oh, have you hurt your hands?'

Mum's hands were all swollen and the little finger on one hand looked nasty.

'I'm OK,' said Mum, forcing a smile.

'But wow, talk about awesome! We've been in a twister!' said Tom.

'It was class!' observed Kevin.

'Never again,' croaked Mum faintly.

'No, never,' agreed Anna. She looked very pale, under all the dirt and filth that had rubbed off the sacks and mattress onto her. Mum looked at the boys. They were a manky mess too.

'I don't suppose I look much like a film star at the moment either, do I?' she asked.

'A horror film star, definitely!' grinned Tom.

But Kevin was always loyal to Tom's mum. 'You look as beautiful as ever, Mrs D,' he assured her, 'but you do need a bath!'

Mum managed a little laugh. Now that they were out of danger, she began to relax. But she also began to hurt. Her finger was agony from where she'd jammed it in the bolt and her hands were peppered with splinters of debris. However, the children were unharmed and that was all that mattered to her.

'Well, I guess we'd better try and find our way home,' she said. 'I'm sure we'll be able to hitch a lift from someone.'

'Why don't we just drive home?' asked Anna, puzzled. 'We've got Alan's car.'

'I couldn't drive with these poor hands,' Mum told her. 'And anyway, I imagine the car is a heap of junk by now. I just hope Alan had taken out insurance on it.'

Mum climbed the stairs to the trapdoor, kicking bits of branches and other rubbish off the steps as she went. She reached to slide the bolt open, then groaned. The force of the tornado tugging at the trapdoor had distorted the metal bolt. It was all bent and buckled. There was no way of getting it to move.

'We're stuck,' she called down to the children. 'We'll have to wait for help to arrive.'

'But they may never find us!' yelped Tom, his voice rising in panic.

'Someone will,' said Mum, 'eventually.' It could be quite a while though. Her spirits sagged.

'But Mummy!' piped up Anna. 'I can get out

through the hole in the door.'

'Can you?' said Mum, doubtfully. The missing plank of wood from the trapdoor only left a very narrow hole. 'Do you think so? Let's see.'

She and Anna went back up to the trapdoor. Mum lifted Anna up and the little girl managed to squeeze her head and shoulders through the gap. It was a bit of a struggle to heave her up high enough so she could get her arms through but finally Anna managed to wriggle out into the open.

'Can you boys get out too?' asked Mum. 'You're both skinny despite all the chips!'

Kevin tried first. But even with both Tom and Mum boosting him from beneath, he couldn't get his shoulders through. Tom got a bit further than Kevin, but then got stuck for several minutes before Mum and Kevin succeeded in dragging him back down. It was all up to Anna to get them rescued.

'Now Anna,' said Mum, peering up at her daughter through the hole in the trapdoor. 'First thing, can you see the car at all?' She'd left her mobile phone in it. If by some miracle the car was still there, and not a complete wreck, her first plan was to ask Anna to find the phone for her.

Anna looked around. 'I can't see it. Most of the house has fallen down too, and all the trees.'

Mum sighed. That put paid to that idea. On to Plan B. 'OK. You can see the main road, can't you?' They could only be about fifty metres away from it.

'Yes,' nodded Anna.

'Are there any cars driving along it?'

'No,' replied Anna.

'I'm sure there will be soon,' said Mum keenly. 'I need you to go to the roadside and wave at any cars that come by so they stop. Bring the driver here so I can talk to him. But don't get into the car on your own, OK?'

'I know,' said Anna, impatiently. Mum was always going on about keeping safe.

'And there's no sign of the twister?' Mum was worried in case it suddenly veered back towards them while Anna was out in the open.

'No. It's all nice and sunny now.'

'Good girl, then off you go.'

Mum felt bad sending out a five-year-old on her own to get them rescued, but if she didn't, she knew they could be stuck in this cellar for days before anyone found them. Maybe longer, maybe they'd never be found . . . Mum shook her head to get rid of the gloomy thoughts.

'Say Mrs D,' said Kevin, seeing Mum's worried face. 'Why don't Tom and I take it in turns to stick our heads through the hole so we can keep an eye on Anna?'

'Thanks Kevin, that would be great, so long as it's not too uncomfortable for you.'

Kevin took the first shift. He watched Anna pick her way cautiously over the piles of bricks and head towards the road. He lost sight of her for a lot of the time, what with all the debris in the way, but every now and again he caught a glimpse of her red shorts and pink t-shirt. He had to tilt his head at a very odd angle to keep her in view.

'She's at the road now,' Kevin reported. 'Tom, your turn.' Kevin's neck couldn't take any more stretching for the time being.

Anna stood at the deserted roadside. She watched and waited, patiently at first, but after ten minutes or so she got fidgety and bored. There was a swath of pretty, tall yellow flowers across the road. Somehow they'd escaped the ravages of the twister. Anna really wanted to go and pick some. She battled with her conscience for a few moments. She wasn't allowed to cross the road on her own. But this wasn't really a road at the moment because there weren't any cars on it. And anyway, she thought defiantly, Mum wasn't there to stop her.

She marched across the road, after first looking carefully both ways, and picked a big bunch of flowers for Mum. Suddenly she felt tired. She sat down wearily amongst the flowers. They towered above her and hid her completely. So when a police car cruised by, the cops didn't see Anna. And she didn't hear it until it was too late. She bobbed up and waved, but the cops were way down the road. Anna burst into tears. Mum would be cross. But all this had happened while Mum and Kevin were freeing Tom from the hole. He'd got stuck again. So they didn't see or hear the police go by either.

Anna was about to take her huge bunch of flowers to Mum, when she had an idea. If she put something in the road, then next time someone came by, they'd know she was there and they wouldn't drive pass, even if they couldn't see her straight away. She'd seen writing on the road, both at home and here in America, things like 'stop' and 'slow'. That was what she must do. She must write on the road – with her flowers!

But what should she write? She knew most of her letters by now, but not many words. She wasn't sure how to spell "Help us", which is what she really wanted to write. So she started with her name. She could spell that no problem. With great concentration she laid some flowers out into a huge letter 'A'. Next she did a wonky, backwards letter 'N', followed by another exactly the same. She finished with another 'A', this time a very squashed one because she was almost at the verge. She surveyed her handiwork, and felt very pleased with herself.

Now for more words. 'Tom' came next, followed by 'Mumy', then 'Kven', and finally 'Alan'. Anna left a nice big gap between each word so her writing stretched for a hundred metres or so along the road. Anna was so delighted with what she'd done that she wanted to tell Mum. She checked up and down the road. It was still empty. So she set off towards the ruins. But because she had wandered so far down the road, she lost her bearings. She was heading towards the wrong pile of rubble.

10. Flower Power

Alan and Chuck had picked up the freeway now, and, without knowing it, were following Jane and the children's trail, although at least they stayed on the correct side of the road. They drove slowly, constantly scanning to either side. There was no sign of life anywhere but, more comfortingly, no sign of any bodies either.

They became aware of a whirring sound. Alan looked up. A police helicopter was buzzing over them, sweeping from right to left.

'The search parties are out,' Chuck told Alan. 'They'll find your folks, even if we don't.'

Minutes later, the Pink Elephant cruised by them on the road. Chris Martin waved cheerfully to them as he sped on to start searching further down the road. But Alan couldn't even manage a smile in return. Looking for Jane and the kids in these endless, flat plains was worse than looking for a needle in a haystack.

Chuck was in constant communication with Chris and others of his stormchasing friends who had all joined in the hunt for the gang. Alan listened in occasionally, but most of the time he was too busy scrutinising every patch of the surrounding land.

The CB crackled into life. 'Pink Elephant calling Mister Twister. Hey, the darnedest thing. The twister's chucked some flowers all over the road up here. You could almost swear they were words! I guess I've just got a good imagination but there's one row looks awful like your buddy's name, Alan isn't it? And there are shapes just like a "T" and an "O" . . .'

Alan, his heart pounding, snatched the receiver off a very startled Chuck.

'You've found them!' he yelled. 'That's not the twister, that's them writing their names! Is there an "Anna" or a "Kevin"?'

'Let's see,' replied Pink Elephant, sounding very excited now. 'Yeah, yeah, kinda. And there's "Mumy", I swear! I'm pulling in!'

'We'll be right with you,' whooped Alan.

Chuck floored the gas pedal and within a few minutes they saw the Pink Elephant pulled in at the side of the road. Alan leapt out the second the car stopped and joined Chris to look at the flower writing. He grinned broadly.

'That's them!' he beamed. 'And they can't be far away! What's the best way to search, do you think?'

Chuck soon had them organised. 'Chris, how about you patrol on the freeway, say a half-mile or so in either direction from this point?' he suggested. 'Alan, you and I will search the fields and what's left of these buildings round here. Here,' he threw Alan a walkie-talkie, 'keep in touch.'

'Is there any sort of electronic gizmo you *don't* have?' teased Alan, looking at the sleek, expensive piece of equipment in his hand.

'Only the ones that haven't been invented yet!' winked Chuck.

Chris Martin drove off and Alan and Chuck separated. Chuck headed southwards. Alan struck out across the fields towards the ruined barn where Jane and the boys were, although of course Alan didn't know that. His path was a winding one as there was all sorts of debris strewn around – tree branches, fence panels, split straw bales, large soggy bits of cardboard – all of which he had to avoid. He picked his way carefully around them.

He cupped his hands round his mouth. 'JANE! TOM! KEVIN! ANNA!' he roared. He stood still and listened. No reply. He pushed on further, then stopped and shouted again. Still nothing. Sighing, he trudged ever closer to the ruins.

Down in the cellar, Kevin and Tom were taking a quick break from Anna-spotting to rest their aching necks. They'd lost sight of her some time ago, much to Mum's dismay. As Tom explained, it was difficult to see in that direction, and anyway there was too much stuff in the way. But since they hadn't seen any traffic or any one pass by, they felt sure she was safe. They hadn't heard anything either, not even the police helicopter. The cellar seemed to muffle all the sounds around them.

Mum paced up and down anxiously. She should never have let Anna out on her own. What had she been thinking of?

'OK, Mrs D,' said Kevin, taking the hint. 'My neck is heaps better now.' It wasn't at all, it was agony and Kevin rubbed it frantically. 'I'll have another look and see. Give me a bunk up, Tom.'

The boys got themselves into position. Then, with a helpful shove from Tom, Kevin heaved his head quickly out through the broken trapdoor, just as Alan was in the middle of striding over it. Alan hadn't actually seen the door since much of it was covered in leaves and twigs.

'Stop!' shrieked Kevin as he saw a boot swinging straight at his nose.

'What the heck?' roared Alan in surprise, as suddenly Kevin's head shot up out of nowhere. He jumped sideways, missing Kevin's face by millimetres.

Kevin and Alan looked at each other in amazement.

'Hey! Alan! What are you doing here?' Kevin was the first to recover.

'Looking for you, of course!' smiled Alan, overcome with relief.

'Guys, it's Alan,' Kevin called down to Tom and his mum.

'Yeah, yeah, and I'm a pink and purple kangaroo,' came Tom's voice, wearily from below.

'No, it really is me!' Alan called, bending down to peer into the space around Kevin's neck. 'Are you all OK?'

Mum and Tom crowded round Kevin. 'We're

a bit shaken and bashed,' admitted Mum. 'Is Anna there with you?'

'No. She's not with you then?' Alan replied, a bit stupidly he realised.

'She climbed out to try and get help. Oh Alan, quickly, go and find her. I shouldn't have let her go, but we couldn't get out and . . .' Mum broke down and began sobbing uncontrollably. All the horror of what they'd just been through was catching up with her at last.

'Jane, I'll find her, I promise,' Alan reassured her. 'It's thanks to Anna I've found you. You won't believe it – she wrote your names in flowers on the road! That's the only reason we knew you were round here somewhere. You did the right thing. I'll call up my friends and we'll soon round her up. Be back to you very, very soon. Oh, I love you,' he added.

'I love you too,' sobbed Mum.

'Back in a jiff, I promise,' said Alan, standing up. He called up Chuck on the walkie-talkie and told him the news. 'Jane and the boys are fine, but trapped. We need to find Anna first. Over.'

'Sure thing,' came Chuck's crackly voice. 'I'm just coming up to what's left of a cottage or something. Whoa! Nearly trod on a live cable there. Phew!' Chuck sounded rattled. 'I'll check this out and then get back to you. I'll call Chris now. Over and out.'

Alan squatted down and talked to Mum and the boys, bringing them up to date on what had been happening. Meanwhile, Chuck edged his way around the length of electricity cable that snaked along the ground, away from a fallen power line. He'd just had a very narrow escape. He wasn't taking any more chances. Twisters really were evil things, he thought grimly. They were destructive in themselves, and they also left a deadly trail behind them in the form of broken power lines, leaking gas pipes and tottering walls and buildings. This building he was approaching looked none too safe. The main wall was leaning at a crazy angle. He walked gingerly around it and peered down the other side of it. He broke into a huge grin. There, curled up with a large bunch of yellow flowers, was Anna, fast asleep.

'Alan, I've just seen Anna,' he laughed into his walkie talkie. 'I'm getting her now . . . I . . . oops!' He tripped over a brick hidden amongst the grass and crashed into the wall. To his horror, the whole

thing began to wobble. It was going to collapse –
on top of Anna!

He dropped the walkie talkie with a crunch
then hurled his vast bulk towards Anna. It took
just a few strides of his long legs to reach her, a
fraction of a second to grab her with one arm and
shield them both from falling bricks with the
other, and a few more strides to get to safety. He
hugged her closely as the wall crashed down with
a terrific roar and a huge cloud of dust. He closed
his eyes and whispered a prayer of thanks.

'Are you asleep?'

Chuck opened his eyes, to see Anna smiling at
him. She didn't seem at all bothered by what she'd
just gone through, and not at all surprised to find
herself in Chuck's arms.

'I knew you'd find us,' she said. 'Thank you.'
And she planted a kiss on Chuck's nose.

'Jeepers!' he grinned. 'You're quite a kid.'

11. Time to Celebrate

It was mid-afternoon the next day. Mum and
Alan were just about to go out.

'Why won't you tell us where you're going?'
pouted Anna.

'It's a secret,' winked Alan. 'Isn't it Jane?'

Mum nodded and smiled. 'We won't be long.
Now, be good for Chuck. He's got a sore arm.
He's very kind to have offered to babysit for us.'

Chuck grinned, and waved his bandaged arm.
'Just a couple of bruises, that's all. They were only
little bricks that hit me.'

'They were enormous,' Kevin corrected him.
'We all saw them yesterday.'

'Now you folks better hurry,' said Chuck to
Alan and Mum. 'You want to get to the . . . to
where you're going before it shuts. Quick now.'

He shooed them to the door. Mum walked
slowly and stiffly. Alan fussed round her like a
mother hen. Mum ached all over, and her hands
were smothered in bandages, with one hand
strapped onto a splint. She'd been in the

emergency room for a good few hours the previous night as the doctors first painstakingly picked out every shard of debris that had speared her hands and then sorted out her broken little finger.

The apartment door clicked shut behind Mum and Alan.

'Right, telly on! It's coming up to news time,' yelled Kevin, diving onto the sofa. 'We got up to *Channel Fourteen* last night.'

Tom and Anna joined Kevin, and began to flick through the channels. But now there was a purpose to their search. They were looking for news items about themselves!

'Hey, here's something about the tornado,' said Tom. Sure enough, there were pictures of the devastation around Roytown. 'Quick Kev, hit the video record button.'

Chuck squeezed next to them on the sofa to watch this latest news report on the twister.

'*The clean-up operation continues today around Roytown, Missouri, scene of yesterday's unexpected F3 tornado. Experts estimate that around four million dollars' worth of damage was caused. There is still widespread disruption to power supplies and transport systems. But amazingly there were no fatalities and only a few minor casualties. One of these was an Irishwoman . . .'*

'Mum!' yelled Tom and Anna, as Mum's picture flashed up on the screen. 'Mrs D!' yelled Kevin, at the same time.

It was an awful picture. A freelance photojournalist had turned up just as Mum was being helped out of the cellar, all grubby and shocked, and had taken the sudden snap.

'*. . . Jane Donoghue, who is visiting with an English friend in St Denis, was out driving with her family when the twister struck. They took shelter in a deserted building, only to be trapped when it collapsed around them.'*

'No, the trapdoor just got stuck,' Kevin corrected the news reporter.

'But their version is far more dramatic!' Tom pointed out.

'*Luckily five-year-old Anna Donoghue was able to squeeze out and raise the alarm in a very special way.'*

Anna's grinning face appeared on the TV to replace Mum's frightened rabbit stare.

Anna giggled happily.

'*Anna left a message to rescuers . . . in flowers! "Please help us" she wrote.*'

'No I didn't. I don't know how to spell that,' protested Anna.

'It doesn't matter, honey,' smiled Chuck. 'It makes a real good story. Oh look, here I come!' A picture of Chuck and his Astro replaced Anna.

'*Anna's message was seen by well-known local stormchaser Chuck Foley who was out surveying the damage the twister had caused. He found where the Donoghue family was hiding and called for help. Police and firefighter crews eventually freed Anna's twin brothers and mother. They are now all fully recovered from their ordeal.*'

'Twin brothers?' exploded Tom and Kevin, looking at each other in horror.

'We're not even a tiny bit alike,' said Kevin. 'I'm much better looking!'

'Rubbish!' disagreed Tom. 'I'm the handsome one!'

'They didn't mention Alan either,' said Anna, crossly.

Chuck smiled. 'Journalists always get things wrong. But I mean, how cool to be on TV?'

'That's true,' said Kevin. 'We've got nearly a full video tape of news clips about us. Will our friends be jealous or what!'

They carried on flicking through channels, but there was nothing else about them. It was getting to be rather old news, after all. They made do with an endless stream of noisy cartoons instead.

'I make that fifty-two channels now that we've watched,' said Kevin, ticking the latest one off in the TV guide. Then he heard a key grating in the lock. 'And hey, here's Alan and Mrs D back!'

Anna charged at her mum who was standing, smiling in the doorway with Alan.

'Where have you been?' she asked, remembering at the last minute not to jump up and hug Mum because of her sore hands.

'To get this!' announced Alan, waving a bit of paper in front of them with a flourish.

'That!' said Tom, in disgust. 'Why?'

'Yes, what is it?' demanded Kevin.

Mum and Alan looked at each other.

'You tell them,' said Alan.

'OK,' said Mum, taking a deep breath. 'Guys, this is a marriage licence. Alan and I are getting married tomorrow. Now, who'd like a cup of tea?'

THE ESCAPE SERIES

THE PREHISTORY SERIES

BEAT THE HACKERS

**A thrilling hi-tech
conspiracy mystery**